On his way home from work one Tuesday afternoon, SpongeBob noticed a brand-new building on the streets of Bikini Bottom.

"By Neptune's Trident!" SpongeBob exclaimed, getting a closer look inside. "It's a fry cook academy! And they're holding tryouts soon for new students!"

SpongeBob couldn't wait to get home to start preparing.

As soon as SpongeBob got home he told Patrick the wonderful news.

"I've been waiting for the day when Bikini Bottom would get its very own fry cook academy!" SpongeBob said. "This is my chance to learn from master chefs from around the world!"

SpongeBob gave Patrick a set of flash cards. "The tryouts are coming up, Patrick. I need you to quiz me," he said.

Patrick held up the first card for SpongeBob to see. "Name this tasty fruit," he said.

SpongeBob squinted at the picture. "Apple," he answered.

"Nope," said Patrick. "It's a cherry."

Patrick held up the next card. SpongeBob leaned in closer to see the card better, but he got that answer wrong too.

"Gee, maybe you need to see the eye doctor," Patrick suggested.

"Don't be ridiculous, Pat. I have perfect vision!" said SpongeBob. "Try one more."

After five wrong answers, SpongeBob finally realized that maybe Patrick was right.

The next day Patrick went with SpongeBob to the eye doctor.
"Hello, I'm Dr. Fins and I'm an optometrist," the doctor said.
"Uh, what's an optometrist?" asked Patrick.

"It's a fancy name for a doctor who checks your vision," Dr. Fins replied.

She asked SpongeBob to look at the eye chart on the far wall and read as many letters as he could. The big letters were easy to read, but the smaller letters gave him trouble.

"Did I do okay, Dr. Fins?" SpongeBob asked when he had finished.

"You did just fine, SpongeBob, but it looks like you're going to need glasses to help you see things that are far away," Dr. Fins explained.

"Did you hear that, Pat?" SpongeBob asked excitedly. "I get to wear glasses, just like Barnacleboy!"

"But, SpongeBob," Dr. Fins interjected. "You shouldn't wear them all the time—just when you're driving or when you need to read signs that are far away."

Then she had SpongeBob look through a special machine to figure out which lenses helped him to see best. "Which set is better, one or two?" she asked, changing the lens inside the machine.

"Two," SpongeBob answered.

This went on for a little while, until Dr. Fins found SpongeBob the right glasses prescription.

Next Dr. Fins sent SpongeBob to pick out frames for his new glasses.

"How about these, Patrick?" SpongeBob asked, holding up a sophisticated-looking pair.

"Nah, too old-timey," Patrick said.

He handed SpongeBob another pair . . . and another . . . and another. After what felt like forever, they finally found a pair of glasses that SpongeBob liked.

The next day was round one of the fry cook academy tryouts.

"Welcome to the first round of auditions! I'm Chef Skillet," said the instructor. "Today you'll be preparing the classic dish: kelp-in-a-blanket. Those of you with the most delicious dishes will move on tomorrow to round two. Ready, set, cook!"

SpongeBob squinted at the recipe board. It was too far away for him to see it clearly. He slipped on his new glasses and everything fell into focus. SpongeBob was ready to get cooking!

As he chopped, diced, whisked, and stirred, SpongeBob's glasses began to slide down his nose. At one point, they were even in danger of falling into his bowl, but he just pushed them back up.

At the stove, the steam from the boiling pot made SpongeBob's glasses fog up. He wiped them clean as best he could, but the lenses were smudged. SpongeBob thought about taking his glasses off, but the kitchen was so messy, there wasn't an inch of free space for him to put them down!

Before SpongeBob knew it, round one was over. He presented his kelp-in-a-blanket for Chef Skillet to taste.

"This is delicious, young man!" Chef Skillet said. "It's the best I've ever had! We'll see you tomorrow for round two."

SpongeBob was relieved and excited! But he was also a bit worried. Cooking with glasses was tougher than he had expected!

That night SpongeBob had a nightmare. "It was awful, Gary!" he
exclaimed when he awoke in the middle of the night.

"It was round two of the tryouts. First my glasses fogged up at the grill.
I couldn't see what I was cooking! Next my glasses fell into Chef Skillet's
pot! Then one of the chefs pointed to a giant sign that read NO GLASSES
ALLOWED!" SpongeBob cried. "Could that really happen, Gary?"

"Meow?"

"You're right. I *don't* want to find out. I can't wear my glasses tomorrow

The next afternoon was round two of the tryouts. Chef Skillet asked everyone to prepare the new gourmet dish written on the board. SpongeBob squinted at the board. It was too far away. Everything looked fuzzy. He knew that he needed his glasses to see it, but after his nightmare he was too afraid to put them on.

Instead, SpongeBob tried to cook the dish without seeing the recipe. He added a pinch of this and a dash of that, and hoped for the best.

Recipe of the Day!
Vegetable Fritters and Salsa

1. Cut vegetables
2. Boil with tomato sauce
3. Add peppers
4. Fry and serve

At last it was time to present the dishes for tasting.

"We have a special guest here to taste your final dishes," Chef Skillet said. "Please welcome the very famous Chef Bobby Stingray!"

SpongeBob almost fainted. Bobby Stingray was his favorite chef! When he stepped into the room, SpongeBob couldn't believe his eyes—the famous chef was wearing glasses!

SpongeBob was thrilled that Chef Stingray came to taste his dish first. Unfortunately, he took one bite and immediately spit it out!

"Wow, what happened here, Mr. SquarePants?" Chef Stingray asked. "Chef Skillet said your dish yesterday was the best he'd ever tasted."

SpongeBob was now embarrassed that he'd let a little thing like a bad dream stop him from doing his best in round two.

"Well, I, uh, should have been wearing my glasses to see the board, Chef Stingray, but last night I had an awful dream about them falling into a boiling pot of soup. I guess I was just too afraid to wear them today," SpongeBob confessed. "I was so excited about my glasses when I first got them," he said sadly, "but cooking with them yesterday was harder than I expected."

"I felt the same way when I was just a young ray," Chef Stingray said. "But your glasses are there to help you succeed—not to scare you or make things harder. You just need to get used to them. Soon you won't even notice they're there. Glasses even make some things, like reading the recipe board, a whole lot easier!"

"Do glasses make cooking easier for you?" SpongeBob asked.

"They sure do! I can't cook well if I can't see what I'm doing," he said with a chuckle.

Recipe of the Day!

Vegetable Fritters and Salsa

1. Cut vegetables
2. ...il with tomato sauce
3. Add ...
4. Fry ...

"Are there other famous people who wear glasses?"

"Tons," Chef Stingray said. "There's Chef Gordon Clamsey and Martha Stewfish, and—"

"Ooh, I know one!" SpongeBob called out. "Barnacleboy, part of the greatest superhero team of all time!"

"But Chef Stingray, how do you keep your glasses from sliding down or fogging up?" SpongeBob asked curiously.

Chef Stingray reached into his pocket and pulled out a no-slip elastic band and a special cloth. He gave them to SpongeBob. "These will help you keep your glasses in place and clean your lenses when they fog up."

"Thank you," SpongeBob said happily. He was feeling so much better about his glasses already.

"You're welcome, Mr. SquarePants. Listen, I'll make you a deal. Since you cooked so well yesterday, I'll let you into the academy, but only if you promise to wear your glasses whenever you need them," said Chef Stingray.

"I promise!" SpongeBob replied. He could hardly believe it! He was going to go to the fry cook academy after all—and he couldn't wait to wear his glasses, just like the famous chefs who came before him!

Two weeks later, SpongeBob had just finished his first class at the fry cook academy. Chef Stingray was there to taste his first dish.

"This pasta is absolutely delicious!" Chef Stingray exclaimed.

"Thanks, Chef Stingray. And my glasses didn't slide down once!" SpongeBob said gleefully.

"See, I promised you that your glasses would only help you succeed, didn't I?" Chef Stingray asked.

"You sure did!" SpongeBob replied. "And boy, were you right. This dish is delicious!"